# Sophie's Pony Tales

## GLENN VAN OORT

www.sophiesponytales.com

# Contents

# Sophie's Pony Tales

Her Experiences from being a Reject to a Carriage Driving Champion

St. Gertrude a.k.a. Sophie as conveyed by Glenn Van Oort

Sophie wanted her tales to be told as an encouraging word. She was born with a physical defect and as a result difficulties followed her. Circumstances seemed impossible. A crisis at her barn resulted in her being sold as a young untrained horse. She was transported hundreds of miles, then was rescued from a sales pen avoiding being sent to slaughter in Canada. Opportunities came to her, but she was not able to accept them, yet somehow challenges were overcome. Her story is one of emerging, changing, and finally finding a way to a bright future. It is a story of being lost and then found. Sophie tells her tales hoping that the reader will find in them a word of hope.

The author, Rev. Glenn Van Oort, is a Minister of Word and Sacrament in The Reformed Church of America. Since graduating from New Brunswick Theological Seminary, in New Brunswick, New Jersey in 1966 with a Master of Divinity degree he has been serving in his profession with a variety of congregations. A number of years ago he began incorporating horse and pony tales in his sermons, both to adults and children. All listeners related to the stories. Many have requested that the tales be made available.

Glenn grew up on a Iowa farm surrounded by fields and horses. As an adult he has been active in the equine community in several capacities. Experiences include being an adjunct instructor of Light Horse Driving, at Cobleskill College, and for six years being a consultant to the New York State Department of Agriculture as an inspector for County Fair Standard Bred Racing. He and his wife Eileen were 4H Horse Club leaders for a dozen years. During that time their three children became enthralled with horses. That condition has been passed on to their children. After years of children and teens in and around the barn with a variety of equines, he started carriage driving with a daughter's left behind Morgan. His claim to horsemanship derives partly from his twelve years of experiences driving that horse, Miss Sophie.

STARTING OFF ON THE WRONG HOOF

**"Headed the Wrong Way"**

From the first day,

I was headed the wrong way.

Kept from the herd,

stay away was the word.

So it's no surprise,

I became socially unwise.

Left to myself,

like a book on a shelf.

Or a toy in a chest,

forgotten at rest.

Apart from the herd,

though that is absurd.

Didn't run with them then,

I was kept in pen.

A recluse mother,

didn't let me discover;

friends, or socialize,

that nearly led to my demise.

# CHAPTER 1
# Who Am I?

"Just who is this horse?" a lady asked at our first carriage driving competition. In writing this the hope is you will find out who I am and how I become a champion competitive carriage driving horse.

My name is Saint Gertrude. That is what is written on my Morgan Horse registration. My friends call me Sophie. I was foaled (born) in the spring of 1989 on a farm in the little town of Good Hope, Georgia. Hope was to become very important to me.

My mother - or dam, in horse talk - was a rescue. Her name was Molly and she was small, even for being a Morgan horse. The owners of the farm on which I was foaled had found her in a small pen behind a house down the road. Molly had been confined there for most of her three years of life.

She was friendly toward people, but having never been around other horses she did not know how to act with them.

My father - or sire - was also a Morgan by the name of Hillview Rex. He had no record of winning any prizes or becoming famous in any way. He was the same color as my mother, chestnut. My color is chestnut from my nose to the tip of my tail. ·

Chestnut is in fact a reddish-brown color. Because of my mother being small, my stature was small as well.

When foaled, the owners of the farm wondered about my survival. Being not only small but having a deformed left front hoof, trying to stand and walk was difficult. Most foals, within hours of birth, can run and keep up with their mothers. I couldn't.

Because of being foaled in a barn, there was not room to run. Getting upright on my feet and reaching my mother's nipples to nurse was a struggle. Every day I became stronger and soon could walk with only a slight limp. We soon left the barn for the green pastures. There were other horses in the pastures, but we kept to ourselves. Soon I was running about the pastures, but my mother kept me from playing with the other foals. She didn't trust the others in the pastures. That caused me to grow up lonely. The spring sun, and the green grass of Good Hope helped me to thrive and grow strong. The seasons came and went. I was separated from my mother and put in a field with three other foals that had been born that year. All were bigger and stronger, requiring me to stay out of their way.

Learning to run strengthened my weak foreleg.

Fortunately, there was plenty of grass and daily each of us was taken into a stall and given a pail of grain. Every day I was brushed and given fresh water. Other than that, little was done with me. With little potential, an uncertain future awaited me.

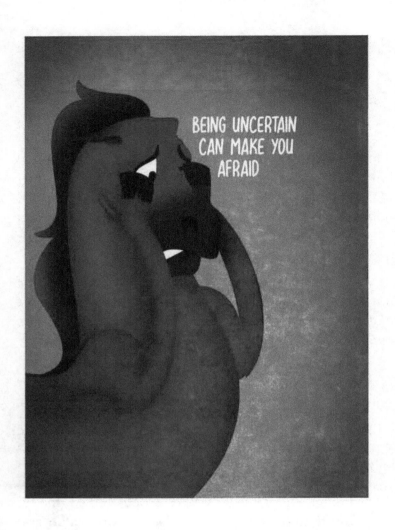

BEING UNCERTAIN
CAN MAKE YOU
AFRAID

**"Changes"**

An accident changed it all,

my mistress got the call.

An accident changed my luck,

loaded on a crowded truck.

After hours of terror,

taken to sales barn somewhere.

Ever since that awful trip,

a trailer ride I prefer to skip.

# CHAPTER 2
# A Near Disaster

One day, when I was two and a half years old, the owner of the farm had an accident with his car on the way to work in a nearby town. He was badly hurt, which meant things changed. There was no more daily brushing and petting. Strangers hurriedly fed me. More change was coming for the twenty of us on the farm. Soon a truck came and we were all taken away.

Some of the others loaded on the truck were familiar to me but not as friends. They had all learned to leave me alone, as I had developed a reputation in the herd for being quick with my rear hoofs. The trip was long and tiring. After a while I was taken out into a sales ring and a man said, "We have here a small young filly with no training. She has a twisted front hoof. Who will give me $500? Her registration papers go with her." Someone agreed to purchase me.

Next I was loaded onto another truck with several other horses from the farm. The same person had also purchased them.

Being with other familiar horses helped to calm me. I didn't know that the person who bought us specialized in buying horses that were too old to be of use, or were untrained young horses.

We were all destined for what is called a killer's auction. We traveled for hours and hours on an even more frightening trip. Since we were crowded together, there was a lot of pushing and even biting. Finally, we were unloaded in another horse auction barn in New York State not far from Canada. I had the heritage of Good Hope, the name of the town in which I was foaled, but hope was fast fading.

A young woman came to that auction barn before the auction day. She had wanted a Morgan horse all her life. Word had spread that a load of Morgan horses from Georgia was coming to the auction barn. She couldn't afford a trained horse, but she saw me and was interested.

The man who had bought me in Georgia happened to be close by. He came over to her and said, "That one deserves a chance. She is a young Morgan with registration papers. She doesn't have much meat on her bones, so she wouldn't have much value in Canada at the slaughterhouse. You might be able to make something of her." She bought me for $800. I was removed from the auction and rescued for a new start. **There was hope for me.**

ANGER DOESN'T MAKE IT BETTER

## "A NEW DAY "

Taken away, for a new day,
Lucky you say?
Should have been, but then;
I was contrary, always wary.
Ready to fight, or take flight.
Made others fear to come near.
Instead of what could have been,
I missed opportunity again.
Taken from a place of danger,
rescued by a total stranger.
My future looked grim but then,
I was taken from the auction pen;
by a girl who wanted a horse.
Lucky to be chosen of course.
But I showed little to appreciate,
having escaped a terrible fate.
Instead I treated her with contempt,
so she decided her efforts were ill spent.
For sale again, at three years old,
placed in an ad to be sold.
Bad tempered, unschooled for any use,
all I had done was give abuse.
My twisted front foot and a mean streak,
all indicated my future was bleak.
Would three again be another chance?
Was this somehow planned in advance?
Was I somehow gifted with something more,
before I had any idea what was in store?

6

# CHAPTER 3
# The Little Horse That Couldn't

My new owner had wanted a horse all her life, and now that she was out of school and working, she thought she could afford me. She didn't have a place for me at her home, so I went to a boarding stable. I had very limited training. When we have had limited training, we are called "green". My owner had never owned a horse and knew little about us, so she also was "green". She spent all her extra money on my board and care, so she could not afford to hire a trainer for us. Ours was a partnership that did not work. We were not doing well being together.

Horse trainers often end up being people trainers. We usually learn what is expected of us more quickly than do our keepers. I have never figured out why we are sometimes referred to as "dumb" because I had soon sized up my new owner. If I was uncooperative, she wouldn't ask me to do anything. If she was brave and lucky enough to get hold of my halter brief cooperation would result. As a foal my birth owners had trained me to respect a rope and halter.

Anytime I had a halter with a lead rope on I would not struggle, but sometimes I planted my feet and refused to move. That especially was when she tried to load me onto a horse trailer. If she put a rope on my halter, and headed for the barn that was o.k. as grain was usually the reward. When in the barn she would try to brush me and soon it became apparent that if I stood for the brushing then she would bring out the bridle and saddle. She would expect me to be obedient. After a few minutes of brushing, which was actually nice and felt good, signs of my resistance would start, such as pawing the floor and then turning and looking at her with my ears pinned back. When we lay our ears back against our heads, it is signal that we are about to fight or flee.

For thousands of years our survival in the wild depended upon our fleeing from danger. Rarely did we fight, as we could run so fast and far that an enemy could seldom catch us. When my new owner would see me get unruly, she would quickly put me back into the pasture, so bad habits developed. The result of my misbehavior was that the future was again bleak. An uncertain future was making me lonesome and unhappy. Without training, my value would be limited unless something other than avoiding work was learned. Going back to a sale barn and ending up again on truck headed for who knows where was likely to happen.

Somewhere in my brief life, a barn name of Sophie was given to me. In Greek, the word *sophia* means wisdom. It took a long time to live up to that name, becoming wise instead of smart. That owner did not tolerate me for long as she came to realize that I was not her dream horse. So she placed an ad the paper that read "Young untrained Morgan filly for sale."

Being a plain chestnut, undersized horse, with a twisted front foot and an uncooperative attitude didn't make my sale likely, except that the word inexpensive also appeared in the listing. Adding to those negatives was having a chip on my withers and learning little beyond how to avoid responsibility. I was becoming good at that, fast fulfilling what seemed to be my destiny, being of little value. I was fast becoming a reject.

LOOKING FORWARD TO A NEW BEGINNING

## "ANOTHER NEW DAY "

A young lady came to see me for a cheap price.
She looked and inspected and found me nice.
Beyond my mistakes, she liked me a lot.
I sensed an opportunity for another shot.
I even loaded the trailer with ease.
Eager to show I could try to please.
It helped that the young lady walked along,
Making it clear she would tolerate no wrong.
I had found a home where I could choose to obey,
surprisingly I found there was no better way.
If I was to survive and find a new life,
I had better listen and give up strife.
Read on and you will come to see,
how I found my future or it found me.

# CHAPTER 4
# New Chance Again

Several people came to look at me, mostly because my advertised price was low. After coming they would meet an undisciplined, poorly groomed, ill-mannered, untrained, small horse with a twisted foot, and would go home.

Then one day a young lady named Glenda came. She entered the pasture with a rope in her hand. Instead of coming after me, she put a bucket down on the ground in front of her. I could smell grain. Our sense of smell is very sharp. An indication of that is our long noses. It has been said our sense of smell is up to ten times that of a hunting dog. When you see us with our heads up as though we are looking into the distance, we are probably sniffing the air. We can smell danger at a greater distance than we can see. People often smell bad to us and when people are afraid of us they smell even worse. By a sniff it was clear that this person was not afraid. She also brought me grain. By having me put my head in the pail, she prevented me from seeing what was going on.

Suddenly there was a rope around my neck. I was caught. Before we left the pasture, she put a long rope on my halter and had me walk and trot in circles around her. She didn't focus on my twisted foot but noticed my agility in spite of that defect.

She had grown up with a horse, but she had sold him when she went to college but now after finishing college, she wanted a horse again. I needed a home and her father had a place in his barn for me.

The next day, Glenda came back with her father, Glenn. He looked me over and approved. Saying something about my having a nice eye, he thought I showed potential and could be a nice project for I was a Morgan. Hope returned because that was the best thing anyone had ever said about me.

They left, and were soon back with a trailer. My owner had said something about my reluctance to get on a truck or trailer. After the truck trips from my birth home I was afraid of being loaded onto a truck or trailer. That fear has remained with me to this day. This trailer was different from the other trailers since it had open sides at eye level. The other trailers were all closed in, so going into them was like going into a cave, which was scary.

After some papers were signed, Glenda took a firm hold of my lead rope and walked along side of me right toward and into the trailer. I willingly walked along side of her. Confidence can be catching. If people try to force me to follow, naturally I resist. Following her, we both walked onto the trailer.

Soon there appeared a new home that had a barn, and pastures with trees. There was room to run, abundant grass and pasture mates. Although I did not deserve it, this was another chance to be better.

**"A New Start at a New Home"**

Found a new place to be,

   but I sought to be free.

So over the barn door I flew,

   in the morning all knew.

   I was prone to leave,

      all came to believe;

      with a latch being smart,

   I could quickly depart,

   So locks were applied,

   to keep me inside.

# CHAPTER 5
# Life At My New Home

The second day at my new home, I realized that they only had small hooks on the stall and barn doors, making them easy to open. After dark, my lips went to work unhooking the stall door. It took me an hour but the barn door opened easily and I went out for a walk to the green lawn and feasted on the grass until the sun came up. The other horses were still in their stalls and not wanting to go off by myself required staying close to the barn. The next day they put snaps on the barn door but did not do anything to change the stall door that was a half door. The barn door was also half a door. It was simple to jump those. So again, I feasted on the lawn that tasted good.

What is just beyond one's reach looks inviting. That can get you, and us, into a lot of trouble. Later I heard someone say, "Any horse that can jump a door like that from a standing stop, can jump like a deer, so we had better make her stall more secure." The next day my stall was closed in from top to bottom with a full length stall door.

Monarch, one of the other horses there, was also a Morgan. For the next two years, we hung out together. He was a horse who also had issues. We became fast friends. He had trouble because someone had been mean to him when he was young. Apparently, he was punished while being ridden in an enclosed ring. As a consequence, he became very upset and nervous when asked to enter a riding ring or arena. Out in open fields on trail rides he was calm and confident so we were taken on trail rides a couple of times a week. At times we would go for miles. Muscles and stamina were being developed. I was seldom frightened on the trail rides, We would encounter deer and wild turkeys, but where Monarch went I would confidently follow without fear.

We would cross and sometimes walk along a road. Cars and trucks would pass us, but Monarch wouldn't flinch so neither would I. He set a good example for me. We often learn from each other. Confidence when out on trails and roads would serve me well later, when I started pulling a carriage.

At times Glenn rode Monarch. They would come to a smooth flat field road and Monarch would start trotting. He was hard to keep up with, as he had a big trot. He would start trotting, and keep trotting for miles, moving at about 15 miles per hour. My rider would encourage me to trot as well, instead of cantering to keep up. I couldn't trot anywhere near as fast, would fall far behind and often slow to a walk. Sometimes my rider and I would both get back to the barn long after Monarch was back in his stall.

Little else was expected of me, making life easy and relaxing. I was always looking for a way to escape. There was a garden gate that people used to enter the paddock in front of the barn, held in place with pins. The gate could easily be lifted off those pin hinges, but I didn't use that knowledge for a year, keeping it in reserve for the right day to leave.

One day, when the Glenn could obviously see me, I walked over to the gate, lifted it off the hinges with my teeth and let it drop to the ground. Rather than escaping, I went back to eat hay with the other five horses in the paddock. It was now obvious that an escape was available anytime it was needed. I was learning to avoid temptation, living up to my nickname Sophie, and maybe even my given name, Saint Gertrude. Glenn changed the gate hinges.

**"Finding a Way Out"**

A neighbor came with carrots nearly every day.

Sometimes others would bully me away.

Thinking of how to be in line ahead,

I would go get them myself instead.

Found a way of the fence to get through,

a way that no other horse knew.

When my escape route was revealed,

the result was staying in the field.

Again busted.

Not to be trusted.

# CHAPTER 6
# Escaping For Carrots

The next-door neighbor would occasionally come to the pasture fence, and talk to us, bringing carrots. We listened as long as the carrots lasted. The fence was six strands of smooth wire with the wires attached to posts every fifty feet. I found that one post was broken at the bottom but the tight wire kept the post upright, making it look strong. After testing it was obvious that if a post was pushed, it would be flattened, making it possible to walk on the post, stepping over the electrified wires on the post now lying on the ground. After reaching the other side of the fence, stepping off the post would make the fence spring back upright. I made my way to the neighbor's house and after rattling the front door, someone would come out with carrots. After carrots and going back the way I came out, I rejoined the other horses in the pasture.

The other four horses never caught on about how to escape. They got no carrots.

One day the neighbor told Glenn about my coming to his house early in the morning for a carrot. He said, "How can that happen?" He got up very early the next day and watched as I went for a carrot. The post was fixed and my escape route blocked making it necessary to wait for carrots to come to me. This was a lesson on becoming patient. It's called delayed gratification. Previously, I had almost always gotten what I wanted right away.

I was learning an important lesson which was to wait. Later when I became a carriage horse, my partner and I would spend a lot of our time at events standing waiting. My destiny was unfolding, but I didn't realize it. Sometimes a way being blocked makes another way possible.

**"MAKING THE FRONT PAGE OF THE PAPER "**

What a day it was for me;

a day for local history.

Playing more than just a role.

I admit it,  I stole the show.

At the head of the parade,

I was proud and not afraid.

People gathered all around.

Children added to the sound.

They patted and stroked my head.

I was not mean but gentle instead.

I showed then what I could be.

A day to remember, can't you see.

# CHAPTER 7
# In A Parade

One day after being at the farm for three years, at 8:00 a.m. there was a flurry of activity. I was taken out of the stall and groomed. Glenn had gotten a phone call saying there was a 200th Anniversary Celebration Parade of our town's founding scheduled for 10:00 a.m. The horse chosen to reenact the delivery of the Town Charter from the New York State Capital to Town Hall had called in sick. A substitute was needed to lead the parade. The town official telephoned and said, "I know there are horses on your farm. Is there a horse in your barn that could come and reenact the historic event?"

I overheard Glenn say, "There is a horse in the barn that might do it." I also heard him say, "She has never been in a parade before so at the first sign of trouble we will leave and go home." He knew there would be fire engines with sirens, muskets firing, and bands with drums. We were supposed to lead a procession of important dignitaries from around the region. People would be dressed in costumes.

Monarch was too excitable to be trusted in a parade. The other two horses were also unsuitable for parade duty. Because of showing a calm attitude toward surprises Glenn trusted me at the parade. Soon there I was, a small, plain, Morgan with a twisted front foot, at the head of the parade. Neither the sirens, the crowd, or the flags mattered. I startled for a moment, when a flock of pigeons flew out from under the girders of an overpass as we went through. A pat on the neck and the words "you're o.k." settled me down. Comforting words and a friendly touch help in tense situations.

Children crowded around me at parade's end, all wanting their picture taken with me. I didn't step on a single toe.

Glenn, who was to become my driver, was riding me that day. He had confidence in me and that gave me confidence. That combination was important and would prove to be important in the future. Confidence can be transmitted.

Next day on the front page of the newspaper paper there was my picture, in color. That felt much better than being in a classified ad listed for sale. I was becoming worthy.

**"A New Beginning Again"**

I had yet another chance,

for a place in life's dance.

A young girl to care for me,

caring for her my job to be.

All soon went bad,

an incident we had.

Really the fault of no one,

ending a career hardly begun.

When all efforts ended poorly,

success was needed sorely.

Harnessed and hooked to cart,

appeared to be my next start.

# CHAPTER 8
# A New Job & A New Beginning

My life's next phase was taking care of young girls. My owner became too occupied with work and other activities to have much time to spend with me. A girl nearby wanted a horse but could not afford one. She heard about me. She knew that I had extra time on my hooves so she came to brush me and ride me in exchange for keeping my stall clean. I enjoyed the time we spent together. I received regular exercise, which felt good.

One day that girl rode me to a neighboring farm. I was ridden in a ring with other horses. I had a frightening encounter with another horse. My rider rode me close to the back legs of a horse in front of us. The horse in front of me kicked out and cut a gash in my chest. The blood pulsed out. An artery had been cut. All the riders stopped their horses.

People came rushing to me from all directions. Children started crying. There was confusion. Someone got a clean bandage and pressed it against my chest, to stop the flow of blood. After what seemed a long time a lady in a white coat came. She stitched the cut together. Even though I was scared, I stood very quietly while all this was going on. From then on I was cautious about being too near other horses' hooves. Even when loose in a pasture with other equines, I usually kept to myself as I had been brought up that way. This experience taught me again to be careful around other horses. You would probably call me shy, but I was looking out for my safety.

Being safe and being comfortable are two important goals for horses. After being injured in a riding ring, I was afraid of being in a riding ring with other horses. I much preferred being out on trails. All I did for a couple of years was to go on trail rides, Glenda and her younger sister Heather decided I should be trained to pull a cart. I was now seven years old and it was time I acquired a skill beyond trail riding.

The family had a cart and harness because Heather had used them for her carriage horse. First I got used to the parts of the harness being put on. The most difficult of all the harness parts was the bridle with its blinders. I was naturally suspicious of what was around me. Additionally, after being injured by another horse, I was fearful of other horses coming close. Blinders, or blinkers as they are also called, are guards on the bridle that restrict rear and some side vision. One purpose of them is to help us not be startled by actions behind or beside us. We are suspicious about objects or activity behind us because it could be a beast of prey seeking to attack. Blinders help us focus on what is ahead of us. Blinders can even help protect our eyes from a whip lash when the driver is using the whip to give us guidance After getting accustomed to the bridle with the blinders, I was ground driven. A person would walk behind me on the ground and give me cues with the reins, whip and voice. After days of that activity, I started pulling objects on the ground. Next was learning to be comfortable with shafts along my side that pushed against me. At first it felt like I had to get away from them but I slowly accepted them. Assistants held the shafts along my side while I walked, being guided by a person walking behind on the ground. The words, "She's a natural at this; this might yet be something useful to do" were heard. A new skill was needed, maybe this was it. The traditional way of training a Morgan horse is to teach them to drive at age two. At two a horse may be introduced to the harness, the bridle, and the shafts, but they don't do any real pulling until they are four or five years old. A new future might be coming. A new possibility.

DISASTER IS OFTEN NEARBY

**"She'll Never Make It "**

I heard them say,

in a hurtful way.

She'll never make it.

She's more than a little bad.

So sad.

Ran in fear,

from a noise not clear.

Caused a wreck,

reputation suspect.

She won't obey.

She goes her own way.

Can't be trusted.

Her driving future busted.

# CHAPTER 9
# Another Failure

The fourth time of being hitched, Glenda was in the box. The box is the term that is used for the driver's seat. We were in a riding ring, which was enclosed by a 4 ft. high wood rail fence. Earlier that day the ring had been used for training another horse to jump over poles. The jump poles had been placed in the center of the ring. The upright posts with brackets to hold the poles were in one group and the poles were stacked in a separate triangular pile about eighteen inches high at the top of the triangle. We entered the ring and the gate was closed. While being headed, the driver stepped into the carriage. Being headed is when a person stands directly in front you to stop you from going forward or move in any direction.

After Glenda was in the box and had taken up the lines, we started along the outside rail toward the opposite end of the arena. Three other horses were in the pasture outside of the ring. As I was starting to move along the rail, they came galloping up behind. Horses are naturally curious and they wanted to check out what was going on in the ring. Although they were on the other side of the fence, because of the blinkers I couldn't tell that, so I fled. Many trainers recommend starting a horse or pony driving with an open bridle, that is a bridle without blinkers. Not having blinkers on enables us to see what is behind because what is imagined behind may be more fearful that what is really behind. In this instance fear took over.

All I wanted to do was get away from those horses coming up behind me, as fast and far as possible.

An experienced driver may have been able to redirect me and gain control, but my driver also panicked. I headed for the far side of the ring away from the pounding hooves at a full gallop. My hooves missed the pyramid shaped pile of poles, but the outside wheel of the cart didn't miss the pile. The wheel went up the incline as though it was a ramp. Feeling pressure of a rein pulling to the left, I went left at the worst possible time.

When the cartwheel went over the poles the cart bounced up on one side. That combined with turning to the left, made the cart tilt further on one wheel and over it rolled. Since I was running at a full gallop, fleeing to get away from an unknown danger, this happened in an instant. Glenda was thrown out of the cart and fortunately landed beyond where the carriage rolled over. She was wearing a helmet and was not injured. I stayed on my feet and came to a skidding stop. The harness was twisted around me.

The cart was upside down causing the shafts to reverse sides. Somehow I had managed to step over the shaft as it rolled over my back and against my legs. People rushed to unhitch me. Panic and fear seemed to have put an end to my future. Someone said, "That is the end of her driving career. She will probably never be trustworthy to be hitched again." Again failure.

FINDING YOUR GIFT CAN MAKE A BIG DIFFERENCE

**"Discovery"**

Seek finding who you are,

and what is your special star,

your gift or your life's call.

Finding mine changed it all.

To be with even the best,

and perform well every test;

made my future seemingly bright,

yet much was needed to get it right.

# CHAPTER 10
# Finding My Gift

Three more years went by. My owner Glenda got busier at her job. Monarch and I were left to ourselves, except for occasional trail rides. Every day we were attended to, but we had few jobs.

A second young girl entered my life. She came every day after school to brush and groom me. She cleaned the stalls, and occasionally rode me. Other than leading a life of leisure, I was doing little and learning little. She liked me, but she had little experience with horses, so she did little to improve me.

Often on Saturday or Sunday afternoons Glenn and Glenda would take Monarch and I on trail rides. Nearby there were farm trails and an apple orchard with roads. We would go out for an hour or two ride. Monarch with his big Morgan trot, would reach forward with his rear legs placed well under his body and his front legs would extend far out in front, making him flatten out. I watched closely his extended trot for weeks and then tried it. I could do it! I was noticed doing a big extended trot. "Have you seen Sophie trot recently?" Glenda asked her father. "Yes," he said, "I have seen her do it. One of these days she will pass Monarch"

"That will be the day I thought." On the very next trail ride Glenda and I, together with Monarch and Glenn, were going down a farm lane at a trot. Monarch started trotting fast and so did I. I was gaining on him. Slowly I moved alongside and then passed him. Was he surprised! He was rarely passed at a trot on a trail ride. Later I learned we were going at least twenty miles an hour.

I received a pat on my neck and a carrot when back to the barn. "That was beautiful," I was told after we got home. I was ten years old, before this special ability was learned. Many other horses and ponies are not allowed time to find their special ability or gift. Discovering my gift of the big trot changed my life for the better. I became known for my big Morgan trot. Even though I was small in stature, I could trot with the big ones. Trotting on a straight race track, others were faster, but in obstacles, requiring turning quickly and being agile in changing direction and speed, few were more gifted than me. A bright future was now becoming clear.

## FINDING MY TROT

I was safe to ride,

But had a short stride.

I trotted slow,

but watched Monarch go.

Then one day,

I saw the way,

to match his trot.

And surprised all a lot.

My gift was found.

I could cover the ground.

# CHAPTER 11
# Another New Beginning

The younger sister, Heather saw my new big trot. One April morning she said, "With a trot like that she should be a carriage driving horse. We should try driving her again." Heather knew a lot about driving and what it took to be a competitive carriage horse. She had owned a champion carriage horse when she was in high school. Now that she was out of college and living nearby, she announced to her father Glenn, "I'm going to train Sophie as a carriage horse and you as a driver or whip. She has developed a trot that deserves to be put to use."

"How can we do that?" Glenn asked. He had been around horses, riding them, since he was ten but had never driven one. He wasn't sure he could trust Sophie, or that Sophie would trust him.

"I will come every Monday morning at 7:00 a.m. for an hour lesson. You will be ready by August. I will enter you in a competition then so you have a goal." The older sister, Glenda, agreed that we should try driving again. Glenn was a little less enthusiastic. It would be hard work and take a lot of time. His vocation left little free time. It had been years since the cart rollover accident.

I was now 10 years old. If I was going to be of any use other than as a trail horse, a carriage driving career would be a possibility for me.

Every Monday we had a lesson, then during the week we would practice. It was hard work, but it was fun. Work isn't hard if you like what you are doing. I liked pulling the cart. I put my fear to the back of my mind.

Being hitched to a cart was different than having a person bouncing and trying to balance on your back. Usually the cart was easy to pull. I had to pay close attention to my whip, as he gave signals with the reins, his voice, and the whip. I learned to tell what he wanted, learning to know the words walk, whoa, back, slow trot, trot on, and easy. Everything was going well. Sometimes traffic cones are set in pairs with enough space for the cart to go between them. We practiced figure eights and serpentines through the cones. I learned to balance myself and make smooth round circles when we got to the part of the training called dressage.

We practiced every other day for an hour. I was getting stronger and faster with each workout. One day as were coming down a trail I heard, "Wow, she just hit 20 miles per hour pulling the cart." Imitating Monarch, I found a ground covering stride that enabled me to trot fast for long distances.

The cart had a speedometer that recorded how far we went and our speed. We usually went five or six miles each time we hitched up.

Glenn was gaining skill as a driver. His confidence in me was growing. I needed as strong leader to enable me to surrender control, as I was and am a strong-willed horse. A new beginning was near.

My future was unfolding.

GOOD INTENTIONS DO NOT
OVERCOME BAD CHOICES

"CAN'T SEEM TO GET IT RIGHT".

Three years after the first crash,

that I caused with a wild dash.

Hitched again to the cart,

for a fresh start.

After months of training,

no fear remaining,

deciding to go,

to a driving show.

Two weeks before it I ran to the barn,

in panic and total alarm.

Didn't pause for advice,

now a runaway twice.

At my fast start,

my whip fell from the cart.

A neighbor stopped by to say,

a reason for my running away.

# CHAPTER 12
# Another Mistake

While we were preparing for our first public driving experience, an incident happened that could have ended my driving career. This incident was kindled by memories of the two previous episodes in my life that were to haunt me. Sometimes our negative experiences can cast a dark cloud over our future and get in the way of our destiny.

One morning two weeks before our first show I took charge in a situation. It was a beautiful morning. We started our practice early in the day. The morning dew was just lifting off the grass. The air was filled with the aroma of flowers and grass. We went into the driving arena. On that morning fear took charge of my actions. I had not yet learned to fully trust the person in the carriage to protect me from what could be heard or smelled but not seen. On that morning as we approached the far corner of the arena my nose caught an unusual scent. It was the smell of an animal I could not identify. Later the next-door neighbor, who had given me the carrots, said he had seen the tracks of a black bear in the woods beyond the driving arena.

For thousands of years we depended on being able to smell danger. When we catch the scent of an unknown animal we usually flee.

Smelling danger, I turned suddenly and at full gallop headed back to the safety of the barn. The intention was to keep us both safe. The gate to the ring had been opened before we entered it and wasn't closed. The open gate would allow us to get back to the safety of the barn.

When I turned and started the dash to safety Glenn was unprepared. In turning left, the cart went up on one wheel, and my driver left the cart.

He sailed through the air, landing behind the rapidly departing cart. In a moment or two I was at the barn door left wondering where my driver had gone. Soon my partner came hobbling. He couldn't put any weight on his left foot. Leaning on me, he unhitched the carriage, took off the harness and led me to my stall. Then he took a rake and using it as a crutch made his way to the house. Glenn learned that day to always expect the unexpected when driving a horse. He realized he had to keep his feet braced against the dashboard at all times. The dashboard is the very front of the cart and is angled to provide a place for feet to brace against.

My fear had taken charge again, nearly putting an end to my carriage career. Again, people said things like, "She will never be safe to hitch to a cart." or "You can't trust her." I had been trying to keep both of us safe. Fleeing from danger is what my instinct required. Not thinking before acting can cause a lot of problems.

My whip's doctor said his ankle was not broken, but it was badly sprained. The doctor advised him not to engage in any activity that would add injury to the ankle. The physician doubted he would be able drive in a competition in two weeks. It would be too painful. Between the pain and the fear that I was not trustworthy, it appeared unlikely that we would make it to the competition. Still we kept on practicing. Glenn needed help harnessing and getting into the cart but he was determined that I should be given another chance to succeed. He had hope in me. I learned an important lesson that day. A good intention does not make up for bad decisions.

"BAD DECISIONS CAN BE FORGIVEN"

**"MOVING BEYOND FEAR"**

I needed to change my ways.

If I didn't I was running fast,

toward the end of my days.

I needed to learn to trust,

beyond myself.

Tolerate correction,

follow direction.

Going forward into the unknown.

Without fear of what's ahead,

In confidence without dread.

Learn to trust and obey,

Letting that be my way.

# CHAPTER 13
# Forgiven

The mistake was forgiven and after a few days practice went on. Glenn wrapped his ankle, put on a boot and hobbled about, but we practiced. Cones racing was the most fun. I learned to not panic when the cart slid sideways with the wheels sometimes making grinding noise and at other times a screech like car tires sliding on a road. At first there was fear that it would tip over, but gradually that fear became less.

My whip later claimed that I would brace my rear quarters against the shaft to slide the cart sideways if it needed to be adjusted to go between the cones. In cones competition at pleasure driving events the fastest time wins. Up to twenty sets of cones are arranged in an open area, usually about one half the size of a football field. The cones are numbered and must be driven in the numbered order.

They are scattered all over the field. Number one may be in one end with two on the opposite end. Speed and agility are important athletic qualities to have in being a top cones horse. In addition, obedience is important. You must listen to your whip in taking route and speed directions. My whip says, "Sophie can turn on a dime and give you a nickel in change." He also usually adds, "She can go from 5 mph to 20 in two seconds." I suspect he exaggerates, especially about the nickel.

The route needs to be driven from memory. A whip usually walks the course to memorize it. It often takes the fastest horses or ponies about two minutes to complete a typical course. Penalties can be added to your time spent on going through the course.

The cones have a ball, similar to a tennis ball on top. If the cart touches a cone and drops a ball, there is a five second penalty added to your time. No one is allowed to canter or gallop. If a break to a canter or gallop is for more than four strides a five second penalty is added. If four breaks to a canter occur the entry is eliminated.

There are some other rules, but these are the main ones. Cones racing came to be my favorite part of competitions.

Preparations for the event began in earnest. Both Glenda and Heather helped with the cleaning and polishing of the harness and carriage. The leather had to cleaned and polished. The brass on it and the cart were polished till they shone like new. The carriage also had to be cleaned and made to shine. My being bathed was next. Loading everything into the trailer was also practiced. It looked like we were going to be given another chance to show that I could be trusted.

A leson that day was that while bad decisions and actions cannot be undone, you can move beyond them. I was determined to take advantage of the chance to be better. I was forgiven for my mistakes.

**"Music Can Make Life Better"**

It was our first event, all about us a throng,

frightening me so much could go wrong.

My driver knew a song can help calm,

that day music could sooth like a balm.

We walked far to be seen but not heard.

The rhythm helped more than a word.

Music that day helped me,

keeping me from trying to flee.

# CHAPTER 14
# Our First Driving Event

Activity started early the morning of the event. Around dawn after being fed and loaded into the trailer, we were off to the Big E Fair grounds in Springfield, Massachusetts. A judged activity at a horse show is called a class. We were signed up for four classes that day. The first one was dressage. The bell rang indicating it was time for us to enter the dressage arena. We had practiced the dressage test movements for weeks.

Each movement in a dressage test is given a score of one to ten. Five is adequate. We were given scores of three and four. The good thing was that fear did not completely take over. My muscles were tense resulting in my looking ready to run away, but that did not happen. My driver spoke quietly saying over and over, "you're ok." That helped keep me from running away out of the show ring. Everyone watching could see my nervousness.

The next class was called a pleasure class, but I was not feeling the pleasure. We were supposed to look relaxed and confident. In the ring there were prancing steeds harnessed with polished leather hitched to carts with lots of shining brass. Remember my aversion to hearing horses coming near me, after my being kicked by a horse in front of me? Please remember also the bad experience when my pulling a cart had just started. That was when the sound of an unseen running horse behind me was heard, causing me to run, resulting in the cart crashing. That is still a frightening memory. In the ring, horses kept passing me. When I heard the sound of their pounding hoofs and the carriages rattling was I would tense up. My back and neck would stiffen, resulting in going "off stride". Once or twice I almost galloped. Eight ribbons were handed out; we didn't get one. We exited the ring and my co-owner Glenda, who had come along to help, said, "Well at least she stayed in the ring and didn't run over anybody." That was said as a compliment. Later that year, Glenn asked a famous trainer how he could help me overcome my fear of other horses in a ring.

He said, "She will probably never get over her fear while in a ring with other horses and carts." Sometimes bad experiences are held in memory forever. Fortunately my carriage wreck years ago did not stop me from being hitched again. After being in a show ring with other horses there was a need for me to calm down. We went into a large field nearby and walked to quiet my nerves. While out in the field, my whip sang to me. My whip had read somewhere that every Morgan has its hymn. If your driver or rider finds the hymn tune that is yours, using it can have a calming effect. My whip had looked in a hymnbook and found a tune named "Saint Gertrude". That tune is a marching tune often sung to words that begin, "Onward Christian soldiers, marching as to war."

He made up new words:

Forward we go Sophie,
moving fast and true,
Keep your wits about you,
there's nothing to trouble you.
Onward we go Sophie,
better than before,
If we show improvement,
who cares what's the score?
There is nothing out there,
that you have to fear.
Keep calm and collected,
for you I'm always here.
Forward we go Sophie,
moving fast and true,
keep your wits about you,
there's nothing to trouble you.

Later I learned how to relax in strange surroundings, but on that day we walked and he sang.

Music can help to bring calm.

PERSISTANCE
PAYS

"**Practice helps makes Success Happen**"

We had practiced often at home alone,

in a field set with cone after cone,

When I saw cones I was eager to go,

and all saw I was anything but slow.

We were smooth and we were fast,

maybe not first but certainly not last,

Places announced, we won blue.

A cones racing career coming true.

# CHAPTER 15
# Our First Ribbon & More

After the ring pleasure class came the obstacle or cones classes. My whip had walked the cones several times and calculated the best route.

I had high hopes for that event because of my trotting speed and ability to make rapid turns. There would be no worries about other horses running into me.

We ran the course as planned. It was smooth and fast, with no breaks cantering or dropped balls. I made all the right moves. We crossed the finish line and the announcer said,

"That is the fastest time so far today of all horses, training level and open division. You may have seen the winner as she finished ten seconds faster than any other entry so far." The time held and I heard for the first time, the words; "The blue ribbon goes to Saint Gertrude." Finding my gift made all the difference in my life. My destiny was fulfilling, and it was fun. We gained confidence as partners that day.

The next, and final, obstacle class was a pick your own route class. In pick your own route, after going over the starting line you need to go through each set of cones in either direction, not missing any and not going through any set twice. The cones are not numbered.

Again we were fast, with no balls down, and I thought no other penalties. The announcer said, "The entry was fast, but they are eliminated due to missing one set of cones."

This was the first of many failures we have had in cones courses. My whip sometimes made

mistakes and I do recall a couple of times when it was my fault.

I must add that only once did we receive a penalty for breaking into a canter. As you can probably tell, we enjoy cones courses. Many times it has been said, "Look at that little horse go, she moves not only with speed but also grace and enthusiasm."

Sometimes it feels as though I have wings and I take flight, sailing through the cones as though they were clouds in the sky. In one event we were in the clouds. We were waiting for our turn on the cones course at President Van Buren's Home, in Kinderhook, New York, a national historic site. We were on the front lawn and the course included moving between and around stately trees.

A storm was threatening. The starter said, "If you are ready to go, we are ready, but hurry and get your run in before the rain begins." We were through set twelve of twenty and were heading for thirteen when the approaching rain arrived. A gust of wind tore leaves off the trees and a stinging rain blinded human eyesight. My whip lost sight of cones set thirteen. A set in view ahead slightly to the left appeared. We went for it, never breaking stride. We passed through it and my whip saw as we exited that it was indeed set thirteen. The rain slowed, he regained his vision, and guided me the next seven sets to the finish line. The judge said, "That pony knows her business. She puts her head down and goes to work, not being distracted by anything." Needless to say, we received the blue ribbon. Hours of practice made the awards possible. Persistence in learning the right moves made it happen for us. Indeed persistence pays.

LISTENING TO THE WRONG VOICES CAN MAKE YOU MISS YOUR GOAL

**"Listening to the Wrong Voices"**

People came to see how we could sail,

fast and accurate without fail.

In front of grandstand was a test,

To see an invited few do their best,

On our turn we were clean and fast,

until turning for the cones set last.

The bleachers filled with applause and cheers.

The sounds were new, startling to my ears.
I n panic I galloped , getting penalties;

otherwise would have won with ease.

# CHAPTER 16
# Being Distracted

We went to a couple more events that first year. Several blue ribbons were the result. All of them were from cones classes. As soon as I had accumulated five blue ribbons, we were promoted to being an open horse level.

We had started together as a training level horse. Being an open horse meant I had to compete against other accomplished horses and their whips. In the cones courses the only difference is that the cones are set closer together for open horses than they are for training level horses or ponies. At my fifth event I was invited to participate in a special class called a scurry. The class was a cones course with only ten sets of cones. It was much like a pick your own route class. In any cones class any break from a trot to a canter for four strides or more results in a five second time penalty.

This event was at a major Morgan horse show. Usually the carriage driving classes are held out in a field far from the limelight of center ring. Few people observe our events. The scurry was in front of the grandstand, with many spectators. We were the last of the ten invited participants to go.

Word had spread that we were invited to be in the scurry. I had never before performed in front of a crowd. There were flags, banners and even an organist playing. We kept walking in the holding area. I knew something unusual was a hoof. My driver had been given 15 minutes to walk the course.

When our number was called and the entry gate opened, the cones came into view, and knowing what was expected of me, I was fast.

As we headed through the last set of cones toward the finish line ahead, the crowd of spectators, sensing a blue ribbon run, started applauding and cheering. I had never heard a sound like that before and it startled me. My concentration was lost and a break into a canter resulted. After cantering for the last four strides to the finish line the judge said, "That was the fastest time of the evening, fifty-eight seconds, but I have to add five seconds for the canter, making the total time with penalties of one minute and three seconds. That turnout finishes in second place by being behind the first place finisher by one second."

I learned that evening not to let praise or cheering interfere with doing the task that is at hoof. **Don't listen to the wrong voices.**

KNOW THE CORRECT PATH

## "Taking the Wrong Route"

We thought we were going the right way,

my driver was to study it the previous day.

Instead he went to a party , so we missed,

a course direction in the morning mist.

That error meant our time didn't count,

It was score we had to do without.

# CHAPTER 17
# Going Off Course

One of our favorite events was in Vermont in the fall. It had a class entitled "Country Errands." The errands included such tasks as putting a letter in a mailbox and stopping to talk to a neighbor who is leaning on a fence. For that errand you had to stop and stand quietly while your whip answered a question such as, "What day of the week is it?" and then leave at a brisk trot as soon as your whip asks you to go. The route went through open fields, woods, and streams. While trotting along we performed the "errands." The class included six "country errands" and was a mile in length. All the tasks had to be completed and return to the finish line within nine minutes. We were the first turn out to leave in the morning.

The grass was covered with dew. We did all the errands without error. I stood still at the fence, so my driver could tell the questioner the day of the week. I stopped close to the mailbox so he could mail the letter without adjusting the carriage. We picked up a basket of eggs and delivered them unbroken to a person down the road. On the way back we had to cross a stream.

My driver had neglected to walk the entire route the night before, because he instead went to the whips party. He assumed it would be simple to follow the way marked with red painted arrows. We followed the arrows that were on a fence row on the side of a field and headed for a break in the tree line where it looked like we were to cross a stream. Without hesitating I trotted down the steep stream bank, splashed through the water and trotted up the other side.

We finished well within the time allowed. During the show all had gone well up that point. Becoming a little less nervous about other horses coming near in the ring, we were even awarded a fourth place in a pleasure ring class. A first and a second place in cones classes would give us enough points to be an overall show champion.

A high score in the Country Errands class could aid in winning a championship. When the scores were posted there was a red E behind our number. That signified "eliminated." The notes read, "off course." Closer inspection of the markers showed we had crossed the stream away from the intended route. There was a second crossing fifty feet nearer the posted signs. Some other competitors had followed our wheel tracks in the dew and were also eliminated. Among those following our tracks in the wet grass were top competitors also in line for becoming the high point Show Champion.

I was the Large Pony Champion that day, because others followed my wrong tracks. You may be setting a wrong path or you may be following a wrong route. Be careful of your route.

TRYING A SOMETHING NEW CAN BE SCARY

## "A New Challenge "

Trying something new can bring about fear,

With challenges that at first seem unclear.

The next step may not be totally unknown,

but make use of abilities previously shown.

If you are willing to be brave and to try,

You can seek the top and reach for the sky.

# CHAPTER 18
# A New Challenge

We were getting better at all the phases of a pleasure show. I was becoming less anxious around other carriages, even in a ring class. My whip was usually able to keep our distance from other entries.

My whip decided we should attend the Lorenzo Driving Competition in Cazenovia, NY. The Lorenzo Driving Competition is one of the premier events in carriage driving. The first class of the event was a blind marathon pace. Being blind means that you do not know the course ahead of time. No walking of the course is allowed.

The assignment was to follow a five mile route at a trot or walk and finish the course in exactly forty -four minutes and thirty -four seconds. There is a penalty for every second that you finish faster or slower than the time allowed. A blind marathon also means you do not know how far you have gone. The only marker is the halfway point. Another rule is that for the last one-half mile you must trot. In the rest of the marathon you may walk if you choose to, but no cantering is allowed. A navigator can accompany the whip to keep time and watch for route markers. One purpose of this event is to determine if your whip knows your rate of speed and if you can vary your rate of trot. My whip is fortunate because I can go from eight mph to twenty mph at the trot. During the final half mile we can slow down or speed up depending on the need to take more or less time on the remaining half mile.

The route was a pleasant drive through fields and woods with one section up a large hill and down the other side. Pulling a carriage and passengers that weighed a total of six hundred fifty lbs. made me strain going up the hill. It had rained before the marathon so in parts of the route the carriage wheels were sinking in mud. I was getting tired toward the end , glad that we had been working hard getting ready for the marathon.

We worked on conditioning by driving three to five miles for three to five times a week.

At the compulsory veterinarian check I was determined fit to return to the barn. My heart rate was within acceptable limits, as was my temperature and respiration rate. Those health indicators showed that I had been properly conditioned for the event. We finished seventeen seconds early. That put us in third place for the marathon pace.

That afternoon there were two ring classes. That meant the whole cart had to be cleaned and polished. After going through mud and crossing a stream it needed a thorough cleaning. I also got a bath.

When we entered the ring for the first of the two pleasure classes it was immediately obvious that we were outclassed. The turnouts, carts and harnesses were impeccable and looked much better than mine. The other ponies were more poised and composed. They didn't show any nervousness. When asked to stand in a row in the center of the ring for inspection I couldn't stop fidgeting. All the others stood quietly for their individual inspection by the judge. There were nine of us in the ring. Six received ribbons. We didn't. The second class was much like the first.

I heard my driver's wife say, "Maybe we should drop out and go home." My driver responded, "We placed in the marathon pace, and the cones obstacle classes are tomorrow. We should be better in those. Those are events based on being an athlete, and Sophie is an athlete more than a show horse." I was treated to carrots for my efforts to this point and no further mention was made of the rejections. Trying something new can be scary.

IN NEW SURROUNDINGS EXPERIENCE HELPS

**"Not Totally New"**

Even the hardest thing has parts familiar,

may not be strange or there to bewilder.

Take each part as you come to it,

much of your experience will likely fit.

Don't let fear of what is to come,

keep you from what you have not yet done.

Likely it will add to your life's fun.

# CHAPTER 19
# On To The Cones

Sleep came easy that night. The rejections of the day were put to rest. I could always tell if we had done badly. Sometimes it was my fault, but sometimes it was my whip's fault. There were times when he forgot the details of a cones course. My whip had forgiven me for my mistakes and I forgave him for his mistakes. Improvement comes in small increments. A little calmer, faster, and smoother together was a goal.

I had learned to concentrate on what was before me and to pay total attention to my whip. He was in charge and made all the decisions. Obedience required doing what he asked. He had never asked me to do anything unless I was prepared and conditioned for the event.

Being in a ring with other horses and ponies made me fearful. When on a marathon course or cones course I was at ease. When having fun people noticed my attitude. People said things like, "When that pony gets going through the cones she looks happy. She knows what she is doing and it shows."

We crossed the finish line that day and the announcer said "one minute and thirty-six seconds. That is the course record for the day for all classes, horses and ponies to this point in the competition." The record held. We won the class, the blue ribbon and the first place points.

As soon as that class was finished the cones were reset for the pick your own route class. My whip walked the course using different possible routes, counting the steps in each route.

We won that cones race. We were fast and had no penalties. We received the blue ribbon and the first place points. We went to the trailer to get ready for the trip home. An announcement came over the loudspeaker, "Will St. Gertrude and her whip please come to the announcer's stand?"

When we got there officials came to me and put a large three colored ribbon around my neck with the word "Champion" on it. It was announced that, "St. Gertrude is the winner of the Margaret Sawmiller Memorial Perpetual Trophy, awarded to the single pony, with the most points in obstacle classes and marathon during the two days of the competition."

Imagine, my name forever engraved on a large silver trophy. It was a glorious day. We had come far. Far from being a reject with no future, a rescue from a sales pen, I was now an accomplished equine athlete and a champion in our sport. We had come to compete among the best.

When we first started competing we were unsure that we were in the right place, but by the end we had gained confidence and the respect of many competitors. Trying something new can be scary but rewarding.

# ADDING TO YOUR SKILLS BROADENS YOUR OPPORTUNITIES

# CHAPTER 20
# Sleighing

n addition to being hitched to carts, which are two-wheel vehicles, or carriages, which are four-wheel vehicles, I was hitched to sleighs. Sleighing is different not only in the weather but in the way sleighs move. They slide around. In sliding they push the shafts into your side and you need to resist being shoved sideways. Vehicles with wheels usually pull the same, except of course when you come to a hill or a bump in the road. With a sleigh snow conditions are very changeable. The snow is sometimes hard and crusted, sometimes icy, sometimes deep and fluffy, and sometimes slush. That makes pulling a sleigh difficult. From being an effortless pull to strenuous can change with a few feet. Some of us can't adjust to being hitched to a sleigh. The runners of a sleigh can make strange sounds. Sometimes they make almost no sound. In soft snow they are silent. Other times the sound is harsh and grating. On crusty snow the runners often break through the crust with a crunch and crack. Whips help us overcome reacting to these differences in sounds by attaching bells to our harness. The jingling bells help to disguise harsh, grating or cracking noise.

The bells also serve to warn others that we are coming. In soft, silent snow our hooves and the runners are almost silent, so the bells announce our being near. I enjoy sleighing. We go to sleigh rallies. When conditions are right, sleigh rides are given at home.

After one sleigh rally held at Sturbridge Village, a restored colonial village in Sturbridge, Massachusetts, a picture of us was in a national magazine. I had previously been in other publications such as the Chatham Courier, a local regional publication newspaper in Chatham, New York. It made me proud to be pictured in a publication with a national audience. The magazine was the December 2012 issue of Early American Life Magazine. You may be able to find the issue, the article and the pictures. If fame comes your way celebrate it. The main reason for the article may have been the antique sleigh rather than me, but the sleigh could not have been there without me. Be proud of your accomplishments.

## "Great Fun"

Some of our best times have been with a sleigh,
making the most of snow on a winter's day.
The twinkling snow and a tingling bell,
signals that we are coming and all is well.
Hitch up a sleigh, put on a coat warm;
take up the lines, head out in a storm.
Don't forget to sing a sleighing song,
and don't neglect to bring a friend along.

LIFE IS A JOURNEY TOWARD BECOMING BETTER

# CHAPTER 21
# Conclusion

Remember my first competition? It was then that I realized that I could successfully compete as a carriage driving horse. From that beginning, I went on to make many new friends and enjoy becoming better at what I do. I was ten before I started my driving career. That is middle-aged in horse years. Pulling a carriage puts less strain on us than being ridden. It has been fun. I haven't had any injuries. At a recent event, after completing the marathon pace and winning it, the veterinarian checking our condition at the end asked, "How old is this horse?" When she heard I was twenty-two she said, "If she stays in this condition, she can keep doing this for years." A lot of equine athletes suffer injuries to their joints and ligaments by being used in strenuous activities when they are young. I see a lot of my equine friends and acquaintances in pain or sore mostly because they were used too hard when they were two, three, or four years of age. For most of us our joints are not yet fully formed. Our bones and ligaments are usually not mature until we are five or six years old.

My whip was aging along with me. He had been preparing a granddaughter to take over the lines. She had been taking hold of them occasionally since she was three years old. When she was twelve she started being my whip at competitions. As a junior driver under the age of fourteen, A.D.S. rules require that a knowledgeable adult be alongside, so Glenn rode along. He had long assumed that it was his skill that enabled our success. I knew better.

Sarah proved that to be true. She and I immediately began a new partnership. In our second year together Sarah and I entered four competitions and were champions or reserved champions in each.

I have told you something about my becoming a competitive carriage driving pony. I have won many events. There are over a hundred ribbons, and shelves of trophies along with Champion Blankets in the closet. I could have shared many more experiences with you. I have told you some of my experiences, my failures, and my triumphs in hopes that my story may be of some use to you in finding your gifts and setting goals for your life. Life is a journey toward the better. Keep safe and sound.

Trot on,

*Saint Gertrude (Sophie)*

# For the Love of the horse

We give them a home, a clean stall in a stable,

taking care of them before we sit down at our table.

We provide clean water, hay and feed.

We brush and groom them, fulfilling every need.

Some friends wonder why, the answer is of course:

we do all this and more for the love of the horse.

The proof of this love is devotion and care,

a relationship which we're privileged to share.

A sharing is based on trust without fear.

But respect always needs to be clear.

It is not a partnership based on their choice,

Your horse must always listen to your voice.

Not just the sound made with your mouth and lips,

but aids such as reins, legs, seat and whips.

Like a dancing partner, following your lead,

a loyal, brave, obedient, cooperative steed.

Freely giving to us according to ability,

Strength, stamina, speed and agility.

All this for a pat or maybe a carrot,

provided without thought of virtue or merit.

Given because they've given their best.

In cones, marathon or the dressage test.

Or maybe it's just being out for a ride

with a friend or neighbor alongside.

Some wonder and ask why is that so? If

you've been their captive you know.

The answer is of course,

because of the love of a horse.

Glenn Van Oort

## Sophie's top 10 guidelines for partners:

1. Always seek to have us be your willing partner. Don't try to exert your will upon us by force. We are much stronger than you.

2. You are the one who makes the decisions in the partnership. One of us must be in charge. If you aren't, we will and that can be dangerous to both us and anyone around.

3. Be a partner we can respect.

4. Prepare us for what you want us to do.

5. Avoid any unsafe or dangerous activity.

6. Be quick to reward us for getting "it" right.

7. Seek help from experts when you need it.

8. Be patient realizing we won't always get "it" right.

9. Always seek to help us become better.

10. Help us to move beyond fear to trust.

## What Sophie would like you to learn from her experiences:

1. Seek your purpose in life. Find your gift, make use of it and joy will be yours.

2. If you make mistakes don't let that stop your search for your special gift.

3. Accept willingly a second, third or fourth chance.

4. When given another chance, try again and make the better of it.

5. Be careful to follow the correct path.

6. If voices of praise or applause become your focus, you may lose your way.

7. Good advice can bring change for the better; seek it.

8. Find friends and seek a loyal partner in your life.

9. Seek to grow beyond fear.

10. Be always ready to forgive yourself and others for mistakes.

## Sophie's Prayer:

Lord, keep the hands of all who handle my reins calm and soft.

Let no one raise a voice or whip to me in anger.

Grant me a quiet spirit, a trusting will, and eagerness to please.

If I ever cause hurt or pain, may I find mercy, and another chance to be better.

In all I do keep me safe and sound. Amen.

# APPENDIX
# The determination of an Equine being a horse or a pony.

An equine who measures fourteen two hands or less at the withers is a large pony. *Hippo equinus* is the scientific term for our species. Equines are measured by hands and fingers. A hand is four inches and a finger is one inch. Four fingers make a hand. I am fourteen hands and one finger high at my withers. My withers are the place where my neck joins my body for you that would be at your shoulders. Standing fourteen one hands tall makes me fifty-seven inches tall and a large pony. A horse is fifty-nine inches or more at the withers. By virtue of being a registered member of a horse breed, The American Morgan Horse, I can also be considered to be a horse. My partner and I can be entered in competitions either as a large pony or as a horse.

We must stay in whatever category we enter, as a large pony or a horse, for the entire event, but can change for the next event.

American Driving Society: The ADS determines the rules for carriage driving events. On their website, Americandrivingsociety.org there is information about carriage driving, including upcoming events in the section entitled Omnibus.

American Morgan Horse Association: AMHA's website is americanmorganhorse.org. There you can find detailed information about the Morgan Horse, their characteristics and origin in colonial America.

Carriage Driving Clubs and Associations are to be found throughout the United States and in many countries. Sophie belongs to two: Colonial Carriage and Driving Society, Stockbridge MA, colonialcarriage.org. and Saratoga Driving Association, saratogadriving.org. Each of them has information about carriage driving, listings of events and clinics.

## CREDITS

The person who first rescued me from the auction barn in Unadilla NY. Her name is unknown, but she gave me my first second chance.

The instructors and clinicians who gave us valuable directions. They include: Jeffery Morse, Robin and Wilson Groves, Scott Monroe, Marc Johnson, Bill Broe, and Margaret Beeman, Marcia Chavin.

My whip's daughters, Glenda and Heather who in a myriad of ways helped me on my way.

Eileen, my whip's life's partner, who faithfully served as my groom for many years.

Abbie Trexler, Executive Director of A.D.S. who provided important help and encouragement.

Sasha and Sarah, Glenn and Eileen's granddaughters, who as trial readers, offered valued corrections in the manuscript, and Sarah for being my whip and caretaker in my final years.

Beatrice Legere, Editor of the 2020 revised edition.

9 780578 598505